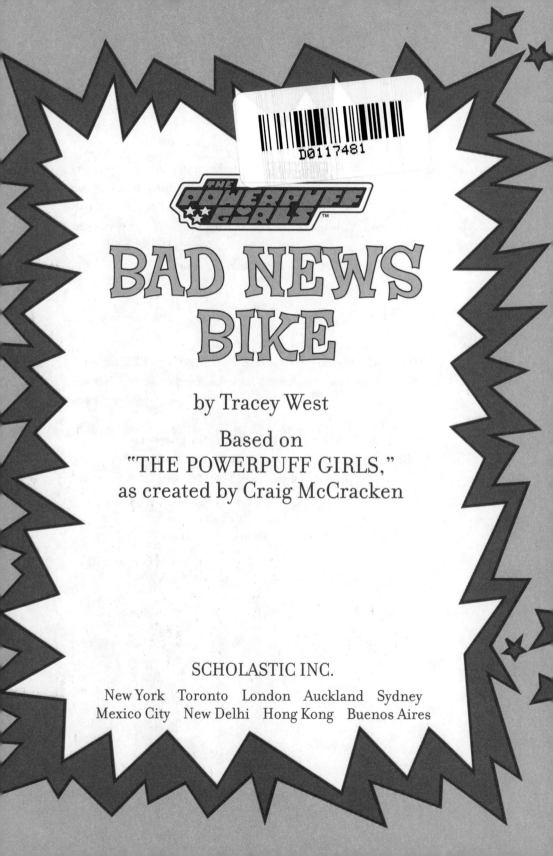

THE POWERPUFF GIRLS™

BAD NEWS BIKE

by Tracey West

Based on
"THE POWERPUFF GIRLS,"
as created by Craig McCracken

SCHOLASTIC INC.

New York Toronto London Auckland Sydney
Mexico City New Delhi Hong Kong Buenos Aires

ISBN 0-439-34435-2

Designed by Peter Koblish
Illustrated by The Thompson Brothers

12 11 10 9 8 7 6 5 4 3 2   2 3 4 5 6 7/0

Printed in the U.S.A.

First Scholastic printing, March 2002

The city of Townsville! Where people like to ride around on bikes.

The Powerpuff Girls could not wait to learn how to ride. Professor Utonium bought them each a new bike.

"Bikes are fun," Blossom said.

"I want to ride really fast!" Buttercup said.

"Do we have to go fast?" asked Bubbles. She felt a little nervous.

"We will take it one step at a time. Right, Professor?" asked Blossom.

"Of course, Girls," said Professor Utonium. But Buttercup was not nervous at all.

"This is going to be a snap!" she said. "We have superpowers. How hard can it be to ride a bike?"

Blossom went first.

She started out slow. Then she went faster.
And faster.

"I can do it!" Blossom said. "I can ride a bike!"

Bubbles went next.

She started out slow. Then she went faster.
And faster.

"I can do it!" Bubbles said. "I can ride a bike!"

Buttercup went next.
"I do not need to go slow," she said.
She started out fast. Really fast.
Then . . . *splash!*
Buttercup fell off the bike. She fell
into the mud!

That made Blossom and Bubbles laugh. "Sorry, Buttercup," said Blossom. "But you look so silly!"

"You are the ones who look silly," said Buttercup. "Bikes are for sissies. I do not need to ride a bike. I have superpowers!"

The next day, the Professor took the Girls to the bike path. Bubbles and Blossom rode their bikes.

But Buttercup would not ride her bike.

14

"I do not need to ride a bike," Buttercup said. "There are other ways to have fun."

But Buttercup did not have much fun that day.

The next day, Blossom and Bubbles took
their bikes to the school yard. They rode
around with the other kids.

But Buttercup would not ride her bike.

"I do not need to ride a bike," Buttercup said. "I will play with some other kids."

But all of the other kids were riding bikes, too.

The next day, the Professor took the Girls to the park.

Bubbles and Blossom rode their bikes around.

Buttercup could not take it anymore.

"I do not need to ride a bike!" she yelled. "I do not need any of you, either."

Then Buttercup flew away.

Buttercup did not get far.

She heard her sisters scream.

"Help! Help!" yelled Blossom and Bubbles.

Buttercup turned around. She flew as fast as she could. Then . . .

Boom! Buttercup fell. Something was pulling her down.

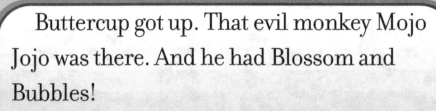

Buttercup got up. That evil monkey Mojo Jojo was there. And he had Blossom and Bubbles!

"Ha-ha-ha!" laughed Mojo Jojo. "This is my supergravity machine. When I turn it on, you Girls cannot fly."

"You cannot stop me!" Buttercup said.

Mojo Jojo laughed again. Then he sped away.

Buttercup ran after them with her superspeed.
But it wasn't fast enough. She needed to go faster!
There had to be some way. . . .

Buttercup did not stop to think. She hopped on a bike.

Thanks to her superspeed, the bike went superfast.

Buttercup caught up to Mojo Jojo in no time!

Buttercup used her laser beams to zap the supergravity machine.

"Drat!" yelled Mojo Jojo.

Then Buttercup helped free her sisters.

"We will teach you to try and trap us, you mean monkey!" Blossom said.

The Girls took care of Mojo Jojo.

"Thanks for helping us," said Blossom.

"Yeah," said Bubbles. "You sure rode that bike fast!"

Buttercup looked at the bike. She rode it all by herself! And she did not fall off once.

Buttercup smiled. "Maybe bikes are not so bad," she said.

So once again, the day was saved, thanks to The Powerpuff Girls . . . and a bike!